ISBN: 978-1547094387

D1410920

For inquiries, contact GriffeyBook@gmail.com

Follow Griffey's real-life adventures online!

www.facebook.com/GriffeysChristmasEveFlight
Follow @GriffeyBook on Twitter and Instagram

For Mom and Dad,

My mom is one of the most inspiring people I know. Ever since I was young, my mother has always had a passion for rescuing and adopting animals that desperately need homes. She has saved the lives of countless dogs, cats, horses, pigs, chickens, among other animals. My mom sacrificed so much of her own life to raise her children and for that, we are forever thankful.

My dad has been the man I have looked up to since I was a young boy. The lessons on life he has taught me through the years have helped me become the man I am today. He is the hardest working and most reliable person I know. Whenever I need him, he is there for me and my brothers and sisters.

This book would not have been possible without the Support and encouragement from my mom and dad.

Thank you, Mom and Dad. I love you.

Griffey's Christmas Eve Flight

Kevin Dooley

To Leo,

Happy Reading!

Kevin Dooley

You all know the Christmas stories
About Santa and his reindeer.
But here's one Christmas story
That I bet you have yet to hear.

It was one Christmas season.
The air was filled with joy and cheer.
There stood a young boy named Kevin and his dog.
A voice yelled out, "Griffey, come here!"

As the dog heard his name,
He turned his body and began to dash.
Towards the young boy he leapt,
Running as fast as lightning can flash.

"You look like one of Santa's reindeer,"
Said the boy with a grin.
Little did the young boy know
The journey his dog was about to begin.

Later that night
As evening fell,
Everyone was asleep
And then rang a bell.

Griffey sprang out of bed,
Careful to not wake the boy.
He swiftly ran down the stairs
To see an elf hiding behind a toy.

As he stared at the tiny intruder,
And asked him to come out
Griffey asked why he was here.
"What is this all about?"

"Please, Griffey, I need your help,"
Said the determined little elf.
"Who are you?" Asked Griffey.
"Please explain yourself."

"My name is Tin,
I'm Kevin's guardian elf.
I make sure he is a good boy
Then I tell Santa myself.

But Santa needs to know
That he is on the nice list
And now I'm stuck here
And this house might be missed.

My mini sleigh is on the roof.
I lost control and crash landed.
Now I need you to fly me home
Or here I will be left stranded."

"How do I know if you're telling the truth?
How can I tell that you're not lying?
Whatever it is you're telling me
I'm still not completely buying."

"I have some special skills,
I can show you a few tricks.
You better not blink your eyes
Because my hands are quite quick."

Tin grabbed a few items
Laying around on the floor.
And with the items he built
A castle with a working front door.

"That's amazing," said Griffey.
"What else can you do?"
Tin replied that he could recount all of Kevin's memories.
"Even when Kevin's family adopted you."

As Tin placed one hand on Griffey's forehead,
They were transported back to that very day.
But in this joyous memory, they also saw
All the others dogs at the shelter that had to stay.

"Why did you do that,
Show me all the happiness of that day,
And then show me the sadness
That still has never gone away?"

"I had many friends in that shelter,
Every face I can still recall.
Tell me, is Benny still there?
What about Ruby, Lexie, and Saul?"

"Yes, they are all still there,
But they are much older now.
I just don't know what I could do.
Most people want puppies anyhow.

Listen, Kevin needs our help now.
We both know how good that young boy is.
If we don't make it to the North Pole in a few ho
Santa will leave without Kevin's name on his lis

"Ok, just tell me what to do,"
Said Griffey in a lowered voice.
"I want to see the look on his face
When he sees all of his new toys."

Tin reached into his pocket,
And threw snow at his new dog friend.
At first nothing happened,
But then rose Griffey's tail end.

"What's going on?"
Asked Griffey with a sharp bark.
"I told you my mini sleigh crashed," said Tin.
"Now you're going to fly me home in the dark."

"But I do not know how to fly.
I have never done it before."
"That's ok," said Tin.
"That is what I am here for."

As they made their way
Towards the front door,
Griffey began twirling in the air,
While Tin began laughing on the floor.

"Just begin to run
And then leap into the air.
I know you can do it.
I know you can get me there.

Just take a few moments
To get used to flying.
Don't worry about making mistakes.
I know that you are trying."

When Griffey finally gained control
Over his body off the ground,
Tin hopped on Griffey's back
And Griffey began to bound.

"Now!" Tin yelled to Griffey,
As the two began to ascend.
Griffey's feet then left the ground
As if the air began to bend.

Then away they went
Into the crisp December sky.
And like a young bird,
Griffey learned how to fly.

Tin reached under Griffey's nose
To give him the minty scent.
"Follow your nose, Griffey."
Then off to the North Pole they went.

As they flew by hundreds of houses,
Griffey began to follow another smell.
They began to descend upon a small building.
"What is this place, Griffey? Please tell."

"This place is the animal shelter.
It's where my family adopted me.
These animals may not live to see another Christmas.
Why is this the way the world has to be?"

"Can we take them with us?"
Asked Griffey with a plea.
"Who would we give them to?" Asked Tin.
"They're not staying with me."

The two argued for a few minutes,
As the animals inside heard and came near.
"Are you really going to leave them?
Just look at their faces filled with sadness and fear."

Tin turned his head towards the window
Just as the animals finally saw the elf.
They looked at Tin with the hope that soon
They would be on the outside themselves.

"My old friends, I can see them.
It's been 6 years this December.
I wonder how they've been.
I wonder if they can remember."

"Benny! Do you remember me?"
Asked Griffey through the glass.
But Benny's eyes were filled with sadness
From all the time that has since passed.

Benny looked out the window
Looking straight past his old friend.
It seemed as though his heart became a sea of sadness
With no shore on either end.

"Tin, we have to get him out of there.
The rest of them too.
If they stay too much longer,
There will be nothing we can do."

"Griffey, we must go now.
We must reach Santa's before it's too late.
We cannot make any more stops along the way.
This simply cannot wait."

Before Tin mounted Griffey
To get back on their way,
Tin's heart sank with guilt.
"Griffey, I have something I need to say."

Tin went on to explain why it was
That they could not take the animals this year.
"What if we gave them to families,
Only for the people to bring them back here?"

"I understand,"
Said Griffey with a sniveling frown.
"Let's just go now.
This place is just bringing me down."

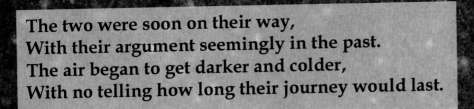

The two were soon on their way,
With their argument seemingly in the past.
The air began to get darker and colder,
With no telling how long their journey would last.

They flew for hours,
Which to them seemed like days.
Griffey's face was covered in snow,
And Tin's face was frozen in place.

"That a-way!" yelled Tin,
As he gave the new direction.
Griffey turned his body straight north,
To make sure he made the correction.

Back at his owner's home,
Kevin was still sound asleep.
Dreaming of Christmases past,
And all of the memories he got to keep.

Then a few hours later,
He arose in the middle of the night with a fear.
He began to think of all the bad things
He had done earlier in the year.

"What if Santa thinks I've been naughty?
What if he thinks I've been mean?"
Kevin then looked to the foot of his bed
And noticed Griffey could not be seen.

The truth is, Kevin had been very nice
Throughout the entirety of the year.
He was always very thoughtful
Of everyone that he held dear.

He leapt from his bed
And ran down the stairs.
He looked for Griffey everywhere,
Even underneath all of the chairs.

"Where could he be?"
Asked Kevin aloud.
"What if he's lost somewhere
Like a small child in a large crowd?"

Kevin made his way back to bed,
Hoping that this was just a bad dream.
While Tin and Griffey continued their journey,
The two were beginning to work as a team.

With Tin at the helm
And Griffey's nose as the guide,
They soon saw a large house
Where Santa was said to reside.

As they approached the landing spot,
They saw Santa loading his sleigh.
"We must hurry, Griffey!
It's almost Christmas Eve day!"

They landed with surprising grace
And ran towards the sleigh.
"Santa, you must wait.
There is something I must say."

"The number one rule
Of you and your reindeer fleet
Is that you cannot leave the North Pole
Until your list is complete.

Kevin's been good this year.
You cannot leave without his name on the list.
Imagine his face on Christmas Day
When he sees that his house has been missed."

"I'm afraid you are too late.
It's now up to you two boys.
I must be on my way.
It's up to you to deliver his toys."

Away Santa went
To begin his annual mission.
"It's all my fault," said Tin.
Tin's greatest fear had come to fruition.

In all his years
Of being a guardian elf,
He has never had this problem
And now he blames himself.

As Tin laid down,
Griffey ran towards the workshop.
He saw a brand new mini sleigh
With a small sack of toys on top.

"Santa knew we were coming!"
Exclaimed Griffey with a smile.
"Tin, hurry up!
This is going to take us a while."

Tin ran towards the dog's voice
And strapped Griffey to the reigns.
Then Tin shouted "Mush!
Only one stop remains!"

Off they went
Again into the cold.
An elf being flown
By a dog with a heart of gold.

They soon made it back
To the young boy's house.
They landed near the chimney
And both began crawling like a mouse.

Tin went down the chimney
Like he has done so many times before.
But Griffey was too scared.
He thought he would get hurt if his body hit the floor.

"You have the toys, Griffey.
You need to bring them with you.
Just don't think of falling,
I'll be right here to catch you."

Griffey mustered up the courage
And with the sack of toys,
Down the chimney he went,
But he could not hear Tin's voice.

He turned his head to look around the room,
But could not find his elf friend.
He then heard a muffled voice
Coming from underneath his rear end.

"I thought you said you could catch me,"
Said Griffey with a laugh.
"I did, but I didn't think you weighed
As much as a cow's young calf."

Tin rose to his feet,
Stretching his small body to regain feeling.
But the pain was just too great,
So instead he began kneeling.

As they started placing presents
Underneath the tree,
They heard a sound from the stairs,
So Tin started to flee.

The young boy heard a crash
Just a few moments before.
It must have been when Griffey
Squished Tin on the floor.

Kevin started making his way
Down the stairs in a hurry.
"There you are, Griffey.
I was beginning to worry."

The two went back into the boy's room
And Griffey slipped under the covers.
This was the most tired he's ever been.
Now his body needs time to recover.

The young boy arose
Just a few hours later.
Griffey was just too tired,
So he just laid there.

But then he remembered
What he did the night before.
So he sprang out of bed
And ran out the bedroom door.

He ran down the stairs
To see the presents under the tree.
He then saw the boy's reaction
And he was just so happy.

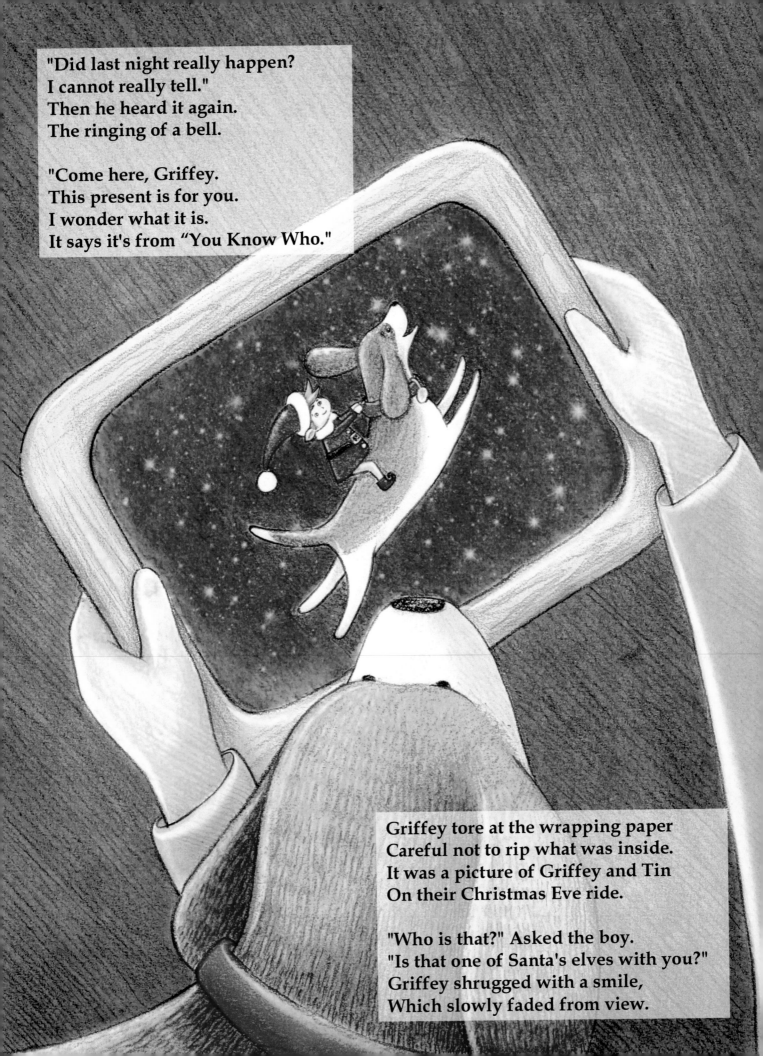

"Did last night really happen?
I cannot really tell."
Then he heard it again.
The ringing of a bell.

"Come here, Griffey.
This present is for you.
I wonder what it is.
It says it's from "You Know Who."

Griffey tore at the wrapping paper
Careful not to rip what was inside.
It was a picture of Griffey and Tin
On their Christmas Eve ride.

"Who is that?" Asked the boy.
"Is that one of Santa's elves with you?"
Griffey shrugged with a smile,
Which slowly faded from view.

Griffey remembered the animals at the shelter
And a tear came to his eye.
They have no one to spend this special day with.
No one to comfort them when they cry.

Just then, Griffey saw another present
Placed near the window that wasn't there before.
Griffey sprang towards the gift
And saw Tin's tiny footprints scattered across the floor.

It was a handwritten letter
From the little elf, Tin.
He started to read the letter
And to his face returned his grin.

"Dear Griffey,
Thank you so much for your help last night.
I hope you are not too sore
From your Christmas Eve flight.

I wanted to let you know
That I had been thinking about our stop last night.
I felt terribly about leaving those animals there,
As we flew out of sight.

Why is it that we are surrounded
All year long by the people we love
While some are alone forever
Praying for help from above?

You were right, Griffey.
Every animal deserves to have a home.
So I decided to go back to that shelter last night
Without you on my own.

You see, I had this idea
And asked Santa if he agreed.
He happily accepted and said, "Go on, Tin,
You have some animals that need to be freed."

As I opened those shelter doors,
I was jumped upon by the dogs and the cats.
Quickly followed by the birds and bunnies
And even the turtles and the rats.

They were all so happy to see me.
Some of them have been there for years.
When I saw the happiness in their eyes,
My own were brought to tears.

I told them all of my idea to bring them back
To the village that surrounds Santa's workshop.
That the jolly little elves at the North Pole
Would make their homes the animals' last stop.

With all the animals strapped to the reigns,
It was truly a sight to be seen.
Being flown by dogs and cats
And every animal in between.

'On Benny, on Ruby,
On Lexie, on Saul,
On Cats, on Turtles,
On Rats, and the rest of you all!'

The amazing thing about it
Was that I didn't have enough of my flying snow.
I only had enough for a few of the animals,
But the rest didn't seem to know.

They were all just so excited
To finally be given a home.
Their happiness was magical
And allowed their bodies to be flown.

I was being selfish last night
Trying to save my own job before thinking of others.
I wanted to tell you that you made me a better elf.
You made me a hero to all my sisters and my brothers.

So Merry Christmas, Griffey.
Thank you for all you have taught me.
I will return to my job as Kevin's guardian elf soon
But for now, it's time to celebrate and be happy."

Griffey dropped the note
And turned to face the young boy
As he realized Kevin was happier to see his dog
Than he ever was with a new toy.

Then from the other room,
Kevin's parents came in with another surprise.
They placed down a large box
And peering out were a small set of eyes.

As Kevin lifted the animal out of the box,
Griffey was stunned at what he saw.
He knew exactly who this dog was
And cried a little into his paw.

"It's good to see you again, old friend,"
Said Benny with a smile.
"I feel like I'm a puppy again,
Even if it's been a little while"

"Your eyes are full again, Benny.
You look like a completely different dog.
Before it seemed as though sadness
Filled your eyes like a thick December fog."

It was true, Benny appeared to be different.
After all these years, his happiness had returned.
No longer was he confined in a small cell, instead
He finally had the home that he so long for yearned.

Griffey and Kevin embraced each other,
As if their love for each other had grown.
And watching through the window Tin realized
What it truly meant to have a home.

68614261R00019

Made in the USA
Lexington, KY
15 October 2017

CRASH! While completing his last check-in of the boy he watches over, Tin the Elf crashes his mini sleigh on the roof of the boy's home. Now stranded and unable to report to Santa on the boy's good behavior, Tin seeks the help of the boy's loyal dog, Griffey, to get back to the North Pole before Santa begins his annual tradition. With only a few hours until Christmas Eve, Griffey and Tin embark on an epic journey to Santa's Workshop to inform Santa of the boy's good behavior throughout the year. During this journey, they meet friends both old and new while coming face to face with difficult moral decisions and their fears of failure. The long and tiresome journey they take leads Griffey and Tin to realize what Christmas truly means to them.

Meet Griffey. He has been my best friend since the day my family adopted him in 2006. Although we say that we rescued him, I believe he rescued us. I hope that you love him as much as I do.

Follow Griffey's real-life adventures online!

https://www.facebook.com/GriffeysChristmasEveFlight

@GriffeyBook on Twitter and Instagram

ISBN 9781547094387

900